DISCARD

DEMCO

The Star Key

by Melanie Joyce

illustrated by Anthony Williams

Librarian Reviewer
Marci Peschke
Librarian, Dallas Independent School District
MA Education Reading Specialist, Stephen F. Austin State University
Learning Resources Endorsement, Texas Women's University

Reading Consultant
Sherry Klehr
Elementary/Middle School Educator, Edina Public Schools, MN
MA in Education, University of Minnesota

STONE ARCH BOOKS
Minneapolis   San Diego

First published in the United States in 2008
by Stone Arch Books
151 Good Counsel Drive, P.O. Box 669
Mankato, Minnesota 56002
www.stonearchbooks.com

Originally published in Great Britain in 2006
by Badger Publishing Ltd

Original work copyright © 2006 Badger Publishing Ltd
Text copyright © 2006 Melanie Joyce

The right of Melanie Joyce to be identified as the author
of this work has been asserted by her in accordance
with the Copyright, Designs and Patent Act 1988.

All rights reserved. No part of this publication may be reproduced
in whole or in part, or stored in a retrieval system, or transmitted in any
form or by any means, electronic, mechanical, photocopying, recording,
or otherwise, without written permission of the publisher.

Library of Congress Cataloging-in-Publication Data
Joyce, Melanie.
    [Dark Star]
    The Star Key / by Melanie Joyce; illustrated by Anthony Williams.
    p. cm. — (Keystone Books)
    ISBN 978-1-4342-0472-1 (library binding)
    ISBN 978-1-4342-0522-3 (paperback)
    [1. Supernatural—Fiction.] I. Williams, Anthony, 1964– ill. II. Title.
PZ7.J853St 2008
[Fic]—dc22   2007028516

1 2 3 4 5 6 13 12 11 10 09 08

Printed in the United States of America

Table of Contents

Tyler woke up suddenly.

The dream was fresh in her mind.

She could still hear a voice saying, "Return the key."

Why did she feel so afraid? It was just a silly dream.

Tyler reached under her pillow and pulled out a silver star.

Holding it made Tyler think of Grandma. She had given the star to Tyler for her seventh birthday.

Looking at the star always made Tyler feel better. Tyler smiled.

Then she remembered. How could she have forgotten that today was her thirteenth birthday?

Downstairs, Dad smiled at Tyler. "Happy birthday, honey," he said. Then Tyler opened all of her presents.

After breakfast, Mom handed Tyler a letter.

"It's from your grandma," said Dad. "She wrote it before she died, but asked us to keep it until today. She asked us not to read it."

Tyler opened the letter.

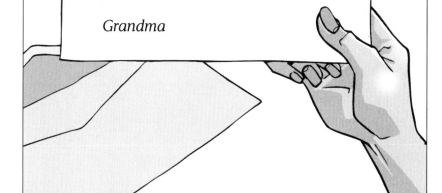

My darling Tyler, it is time for you to know who you really are. The Earth is in danger. Evil powers will soon take it over completely. Now that you are 13, it is your job to stop them.

The silver star I gave you is very special. It is a key. Go to the stone circle at Castle Tor tonight. Put the key on the altar stone. Altea will help you.

Do not tell anyone. Hurry, my darling. There isn't much time.

Grandma

Tyler read the letter again. She thought about her dream.

Did someone want the star key? Who was Altea? What would happen at the stone circle?

It was time to find out.

Chapter 2

That evening, Tyler secretly left the house. She took her backpack and a map. It was two hundred miles to the stone circle. She could take the bus.

But what about her parents?

They would know she was missing. Tyler had to think of something.

She sent her sister a text message:

```
Can you cover for me tonight?
```

The phone beeped in reply.

Got a hot date?

Tyler laughed. She kept walking down the hill. The station wasn't far.

Tyler didn't see the two figures that were following her. She crossed the road. Her phone beeped. She thought it would be her sister again, but it wasn't.

We know who you are.

Tyler froze. She looked around. There were lots of people. Was someone watching her?

A woman was standing across the street. She was tall and dressed in black. Next to her was a small man. They stared and didn't move.

Tyler felt nervous.

The woman raised her hand. The phone beeped again.

Give it to us.

Tyler knew she had to run. She raced past the station, down the hill, and into town.

Saturday shoppers filled the streets. She pushed through the crowds. Then she looked back. The tall woman was following her. Where could Tyler run?

At the corner, Tyler looked back again. Suddenly she tripped and fell. Hands grabbed at her. She tried to get away, but there was no escape.

"It's all right," said a woman's voice. "I'm Altea."

Tyler looked up at the woman. She had short red hair, large green eyes, and a face you could trust. "Come on," said Altea. "This way."

Chapter 3

The pair ran to a parking lot. Altea opened the door of a car. They got in and locked the doors.

"I'm sorry I frightened you," said Altea. "I had to make sure you were safe. The evil Power knows who you are. It wants to stop you. We have to put the key in the stone at sunrise."

"Two people were following me," Tyler said. "They knew my cell phone number."

"They are runners," replied Altea. "They are ordinary people who are controlled by the Power. They have no idea what they are doing. Only you can save them from the Power."

Tyler was silent. She felt scared. Then another message came.

> Don't run.

Altea drove off.

They headed for the highway.

The sun was sinking in the sky. Soon it would be dark. It was going to be a long night.

Chapter 4

Trapped

As they headed north, it began to rain. Drops hit the windshield. The roads became narrow and dark. There were no streetlights.

It was pitch black outside. Tyler and Altea had been driving for hours.

Tyler was exhausted. There had been no more text messages. Maybe they were safe. Before long, Tyler fell asleep.

Then the dream came again. The voice was louder. It seemed to be coming closer. Tyler's phone beeped and she woke up suddenly.

We're coming.

Suddenly a horn honked. Headlights flashed in the mirror.

Someone was behind them.

It was a huge SUV. The windows were black. "It's them!" Tyler cried.

"Hold on!" said Altea. But it was too late. The tires spun and the car slid off the wet road. There was a loud crunch of metal. They had landed in a ditch.

Altea was stuck. "It's my leg," she groaned. "I think it is trapped."

Tyler leaned over to help.

"Come on," she said. "I'll get you out."

But Altea put her hand up. "Tyler, you have to keep going," she said. "Find the stones. Use the key."

Tyler didn't want to leave, but there was no other way. She had to reach the stones before sunrise.

Chapter 5

Lost and Found

Tyler climbed out of the car. She looked around. Which way would the stones be? It was so dark.

The star key was in her pocket. It felt cool and smooth. Tyler suddenly felt stronger. She went up to the top of the ditch. Her feet slid in the mud, but the key seemed to pull her forward.

She walked into the darkness, but there were sharp rocks in her way.

Tyler tripped and fell. She dropped the key. She quickly felt around in the grass for it. She couldn't find it. What was she going to do? Without the key, all was lost. Tyler had failed.

Just then something shiny caught her eye. Tyler reached down. A bright shape lay in the grass.

It was the star key!

Then there was a noise. Tyler quickly looked up. A few feet in front of her was a huge circle of stones. How had she not seen it before?

There were thirteen giant stones. The largest stone was at the center.

Tyler made her way into the circle.

At the center of the circle, the huge altar stone lay on its side. At one end there was a hole. It was shaped just like the star key.

Then Tyler knew what to do.

She pulled the key from her pocket and started to put it into the stone.

In the shadows, something moved.

Light and Dark

"Stop," said a voice.

Tyler froze. A figure stepped out from behind a stone. It was the woman who had been following Tyler.

She looked pale and her eyes were blank. Beside her stood the small man.

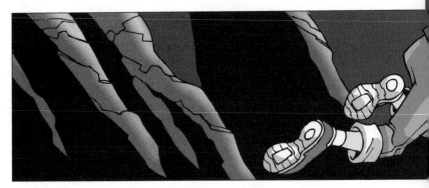

The woman took a few steps forward. She reached out her hand. When she spoke, her voice was low. "Give it to me," she said.

Tyler had come too far to give up now. "If you want it, come and get it," Tyler said.

The woman raised her hand higher.

Tyler felt like something was pressing down on her. She tried to scream, but she could not move. Somehow, the woman was trapping her.

The Power pushed her down. Tyler fell to her knees. She dropped the key.

The man stepped forward. He moved like a robot. Tyler could see that the man's eyes were blank too.

The man took the key. He stepped back toward the woman.

Tyler couldn't move. She couldn't believe it. Had she really failed?

Suddenly there was a scream. The man fell forward. The star key dropped to the ground.

Behind him, Altea walked slowly into the circle.

Chapter 7

The Power

Over the hill, the sun was beginning to rise. The pale woman turned. She fixed her angry eyes on Altea.

As she did, Tyler was released from her grip.

"Get the key," screamed Altea.

Tyler ran forward. She grabbed the star key.

Altea fought with the woman. "Hurry!" she cried.

Tyler had to act quickly. She ran toward the big stone.

With shaking hands, she put the key in the hole shaped like a star.

It fit perfectly.

Tyler turned the key.

Everything seemed to stop.

Everything was silent. Then a soft hum started. It grew louder. Tyler could feel it in her feet. Soon, the hum was a roar. It seemed to shake the stones.

The pale woman held her ears. She sank to her knees. "Stop!" she wailed.

The small man looked blank. Outside the circle, Altea lay still.

Tyler could not move. It was like being in a dream. On the altar stone, the key lit up. Then the stones began to glow.

Tyler closed her eyes. Light was all around her. It lit up her body. Then she opened her eyes.

Tyler had destroyed the Power. She knew what to do.

Chapter 8

Endings and Beginnings

Tyler walked slowly toward the strange woman. She reached down and took the woman's head in her hands.

Dull eyes stared up at her.

Tyler looked deep into them. She wanted the woman to not be hurt.

A look of fear flashed across the woman's face. Then it passed. The woman's body fell down, but she was not dead.

After a while the woman opened her eyes. "Where am I?" she asked. "Who are you?"

"I'll explain later," said Tyler. She went to help the man.

Soon he was awake too. Like the woman, he didn't remember anything.

At the edge of the circle of stones, Altea got to her feet. Behind her, the sun rose in the sky.

The darkness was gone. A new day had begun.

"Come on," said Altea. "It's time to go home."

Tyler thought about home. It meant good things. Seeing Mom and Dad. Going to school. Hanging out with her friends. Normal things.

But nothing would ever be normal again. Now Tyler knew who she really was.

This adventure might have ended, but her new life was just beginning.

About the Author

Melanie Joyce was born and raised in Nottingham, England. She started her professional life as a children's book editor. After eight years, she left that job to become a freelance writer in 2001. Since then, she has written over fifty books for children of all ages, ranging from pre-school to early teens.

About the Illustrator

Anthony Williams has been creating comic strips, cartoons, and illustrations for books for more than 20 years. He has worked on Spider-Man, X-Men, Superman, Batman, the Flintstones, and Scooby Doo comics. He has even done artwork for McDonald's! Williams currently lives in Wales, on the west coast of Great Britain.

Glossary

adventure (ad-VEN-chur)—an exciting or dangerous experience

altar (AWL-tur)—a large table, sometimes used for special religious events

blank (BLANGK)—empty, or showing nothing

evil (EE-vuhl)—wicked and cruel

exhausted (eg-ZAWST-id)—very tired

narrow (NARE-oh)—not wide, small

nervous (NER-vuhss)—fearful or timid

pale (PAYL)—not bright in color, white

Power (POW-uhr)—in this book, a force that can control people

trust (TRUHST)—if you trust someone, you believe that he or she is honest and reliable

windshield (WIND-sheeld)—the window of strong glass in the front of a car or truck. The windshield protects the people inside from wind and dirt.

Discussion Questions

1. Why did Tyler's grandma write her the letter? How do you think she knew that Tyler was special?

2. Tyler's parents haven't read the letter, and Tyler doesn't tell them about what she has to do. Do you think that was the right thing for her to do? How would you have handled it? Talk about it.

3. Why do you think the strange events in this book happened on Tyler's thirteenth birthday?

Writing Prompts

1. Tyler's life will never be normal again. If you were in Tyler's situation, what would you miss about your old, "normal" life? Which friends would you miss the most? What activity would you miss? Make a list of things you would miss if your life were turned upside down like Tyler's.

2. In this book, Tyler remembers her grandma when she holds the silver star that her grandma gave her. Do you have any mementos of people you miss? What are some ways to remember people who aren't with you anymore? Write about it.

3. Tyler's star key has a secret power. Imagine that one of your keepsakes has a secret power. What is the object? What is its power? Write a description of what it is and what it does.

Internet Sites

Do you want to know more about subjects related to this book? Or are you interested in learning about other topics? Then check out FactHound, a fun, easy way to find Internet sites.

Our investigative staff has already sniffed out great sites for you!

Here's how to use FactHound:

1. Visit *www.facthound.com*

2. Select your grade level.

3. To learn more about subjects related to this book, type in the book's ISBN number: **9781434204721**.

4. Click the **Fetch It** button.

FactHound will fetch the best Internet sites for you!